THE TWO STUBBORN PIRATES

Written by Oakley Graham

Illustrated by Kimberley Scott

TOP THAT

Licensed exclusively to Top That Publishing Ltd
Tide Mill Way, Woodbridge, Suffolk, IP12 1AP, UK
www.topthatpublishing.com
Copyright © 2014 Tide Mill Media
All rights reserved
0 2 4 6 8 9 7 5 3 1
Printed and bound in China

ISBN 978-1-78244-912-6

A catalogue record for this book is available from the British Library

'For my own stubborn little pirates, Noah and Oakie.'
Oakley Graham

On their ships' masts were black flags as dark as the grave,
Striking fear and terror as they sailed through the waves.

This is the tale of two stubborn pirates who just didn't get on,
And their fight is remembered in this pirate shanty song.

Bluebeard owned a map which led to lots of pirate treasure;
More than enough gold and jewels for a life full of pleasure.

Crafty Redbeard stole the map in the dead of the night,
So Bluebeard set sail after him, determined to fight!

'Clear the decks!' fearsome Bluebeard declared;
'Get the boarding-axe sharpened, the cutlasses bared!

Set the cannons ready,
and then quickly bring to me,
The fuse for the cannons,
and the powder-room key!'

Bluebeard's ship was closing in as
Redbeard battled against the tide.
'We'll blow them all to smithereens!
There's nowhere for them to hide!'

For the two stubborn pirates
this really wasn't a game.
Bluebeard ordered his pirates
to get ready and take aim!

'Open the hatches, light the fuses and away with the faint-hearted.'
Bluebeard's fearsome pirate crew prepared to get the battle started!

Pirates loaded the cannons in the gloomy darkness below deck,
While Bluebeard poked and prodded an angry boil on his neck.

And it's down, down, sink them all down!

Redbeard sensed he was in danger and made a starboard turn,
As cannonballs flew through the air and whistled past the stern.

And it's down, down, sink them all down!

Side by side the ships sailed; both crews calling their war cry,
As the stubborn pirates stood on deck, their cutlasses held high.

'I want my treasure map back!' angry Bluebeard declared.
Redbeard cried, 'Come and get it, unless you're too scared!'

The pirates fought day and night, until both ships were alight.
And when the ships began to sink, they continued with their fight.

On their ships' masts were black flags as dark as the grave,
Striking fear and terror as they sailed through the waves.
This is the tale of two stubborn pirates who just didn't get on.

Down in Davy Jones' locker, their fight still carries on …

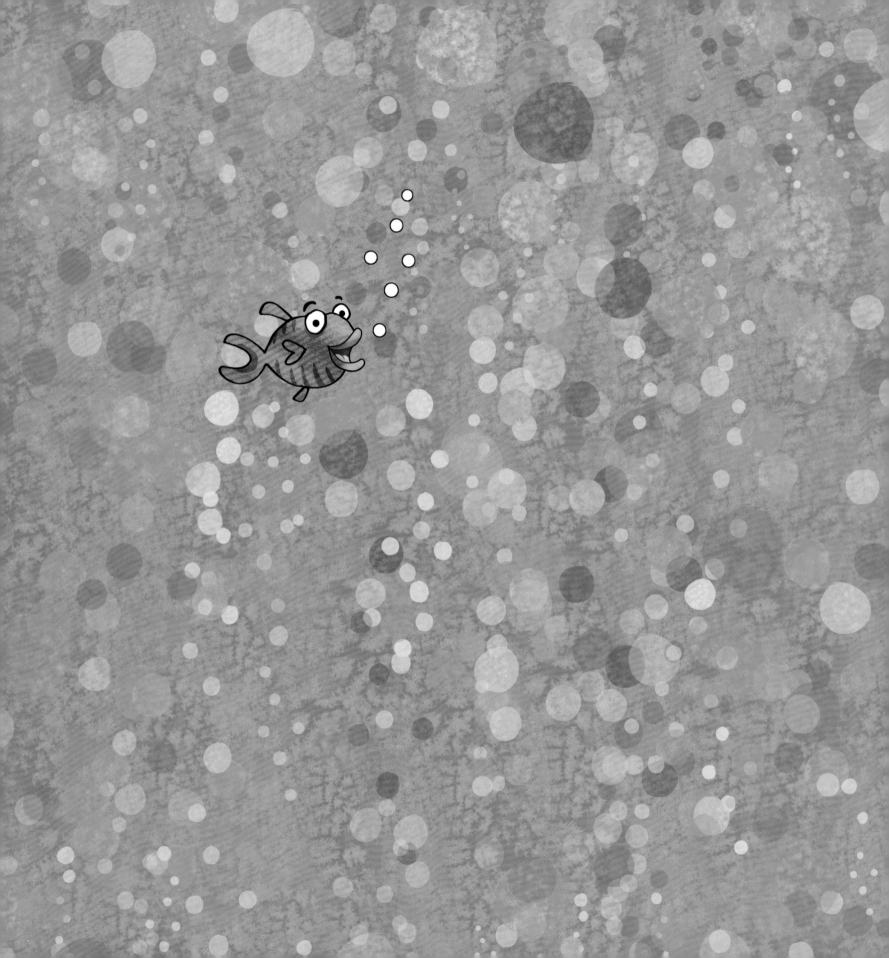

Lesson 10

There are about a thousand things
I'm not allowed to do;
Most everything I'm fondest of
I'm told is wrong – are you?

They say, 'Please don't do that, my child!'
They say, 'You mustn't, dear!'
I hope sometime I'll learn what's right,
For now, I've no idea!

Lesson 9

When you are fetching bread, I trust
You never nibble at the crust.

When in the kitchen, do you linger,
And pinch the cookies with your finger?

Or do you peck the frosted cake?
Don't do it, please, for goodness sake!

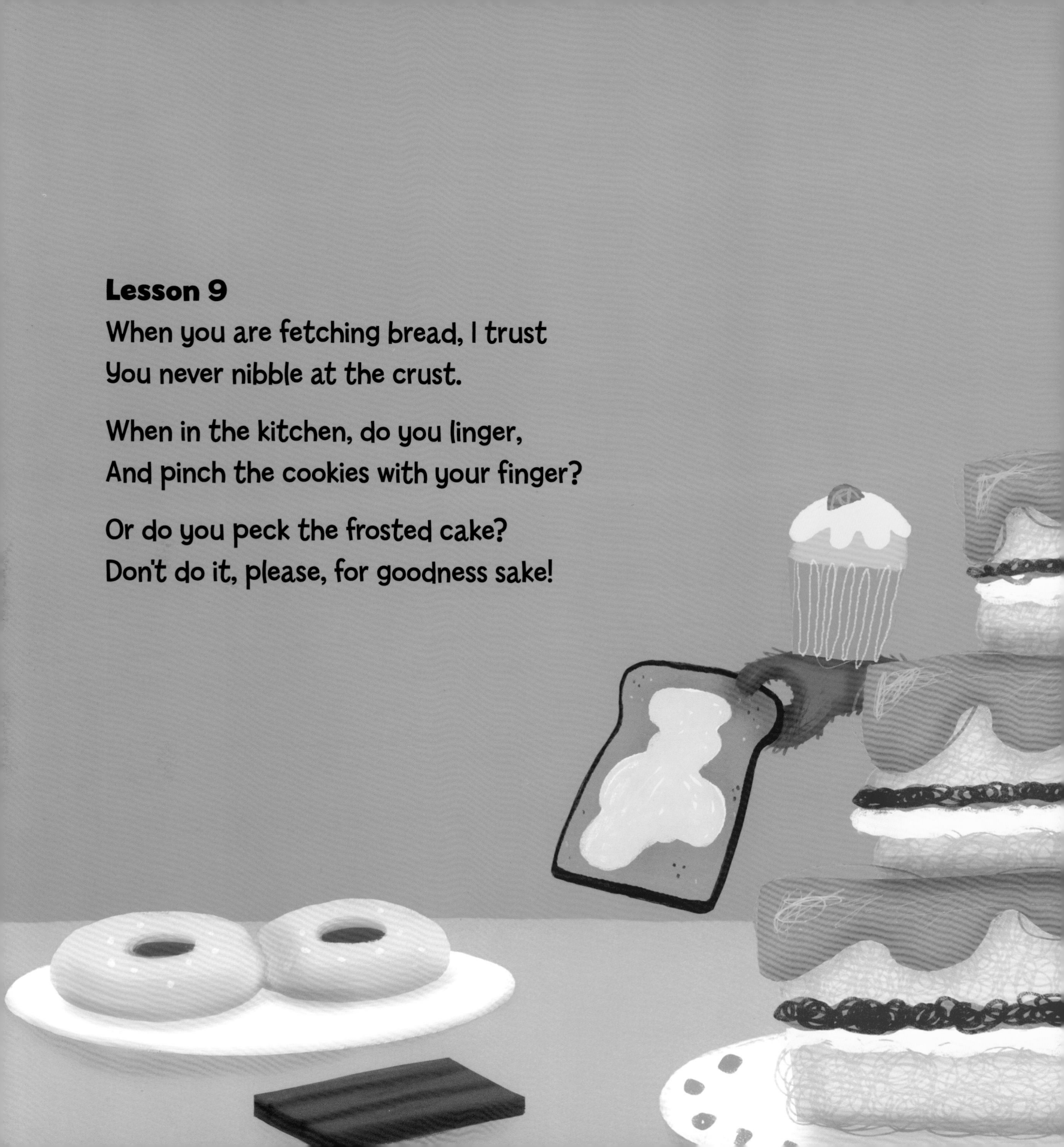

Lesson 8

Whenever you are eating soup
Remember not to be a Goop!
And if you think to say this rhyme,
Perhaps it will help you every time:

Like little boats that set out to sea,
I push my spoon AWAY from me;
I do not tilt my dish, nor scrape
The last few drops, like a hungry ape!

Like little boats that, almost filled,
Come back without their cargoes spilled,
My spoon sails gently to my lips,
Unloading from the SIDE, like ships.

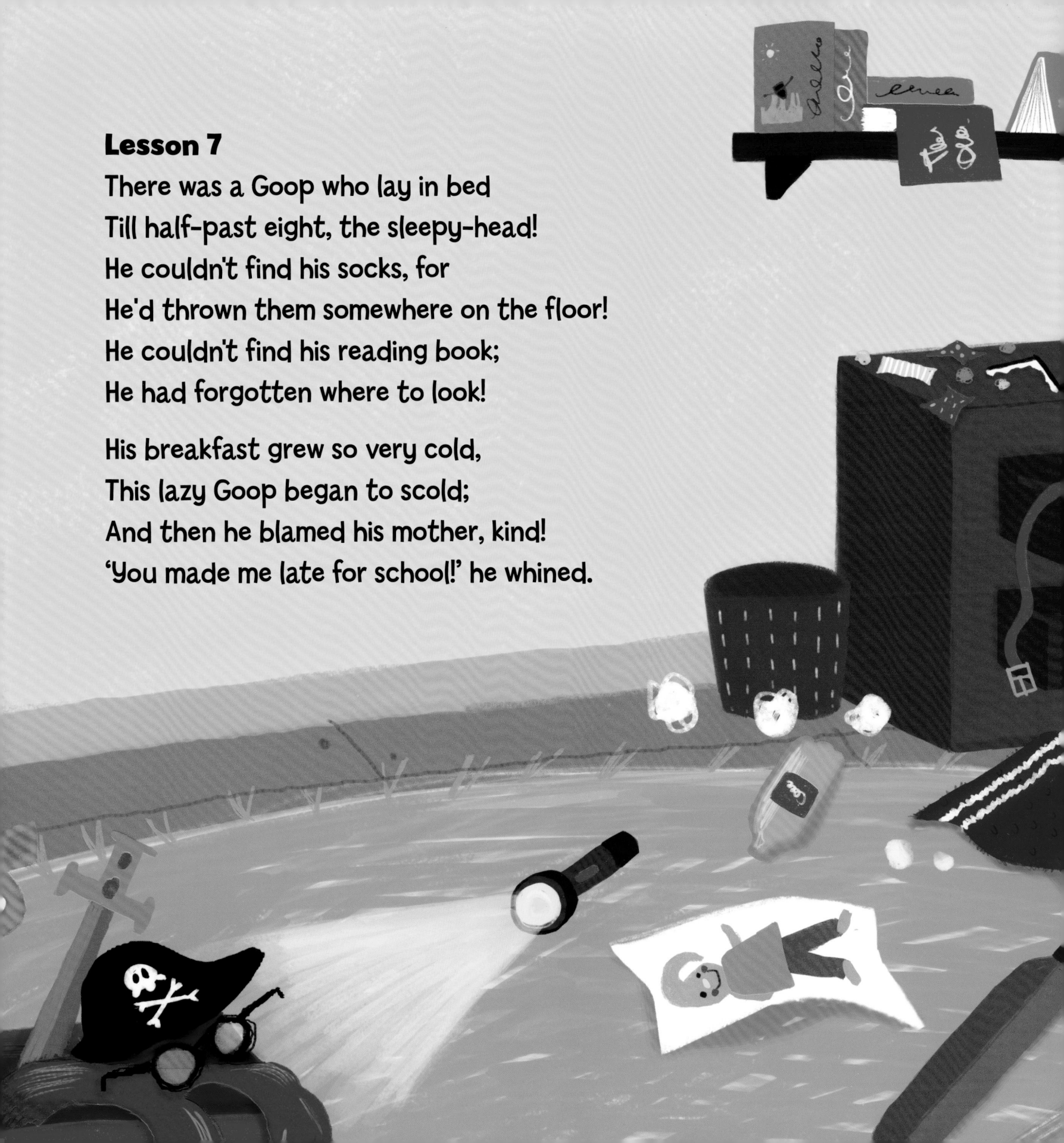

Lesson 7

There was a Goop who lay in bed
Till half-past eight, the sleepy-head!
He couldn't find his socks, for
He'd thrown them somewhere on the floor!
He couldn't find his reading book;
He had forgotten where to look!

His breakfast grew so very cold,
This lazy Goop began to scold;
And then he blamed his mother, kind!
'You made me late for school!' he whined.

Lesson 6

Don't try to tell a story
To beat the one you've heard;
For if you try, you're bound to lie,
And that would be absurd!

Don't try to be more funny
Than anyone in school;
For if you're not, they'll laugh a lot,
And think you are a fool!

Lesson 5

Goop! Goop! Goop!
I wish you'd wash your face!
Goop! Goop! Goop!
Your hands are a disgrace!
Goop! Goop! Goop!
Put things back in their place!
I wish you were polite,
Instead of a
Goop! Goop! Goop!

Why do they play with food, and bite
Such awful mouthfuls? Is it right?
Why do they tilt back in their chairs?
Because they're Goops! So no one cares!

Lesson 4

Why is it Goops must always wish
To touch each apple in the dish?
Why do they never neatly fold
Their napkins until they are told?

Lesson 3

There once was a Goop (it is hard to believe
Such unpleasant behaviour of you!)
Who was always wiping his nose on his sleeve;
I hope that this Goop wasn't you!

He was always spitting (for fun, I suppose),
I couldn't believe it of you!
And putting his fingers up into his nose;
I KNOW that this Goop wasn't YOU!

Clattering down the stairs,
Storming through the hall,
Pounding floors, upsetting chairs.
Do you think anyone cares
For your noise, at all?

Lesson 2

Do you slam the door?
Do you drag your feet?
Making noise enough for four
Hundred thousand Goops, or more,
Tearing up the street.

The little Goop who's greedy
Does it every day,
Like a little puppy,
Hiding bones away!

Lesson 1
Candy in the cushions
Of the easy chair;
Raisins in the sofa -
How did they get there?

Don't be a Goop!

Children, although you might expect
My manners to be quite correct
(For since I fancy I can teach,
I ought to practise what I preach).
It's true that I have often braved
My mother's wrath, and misbehaved!
And almost every single rule
I broke, before I went to school!
For that is how I learnt the way
To teach you etiquette today.
So when you chance to take a look
At all the lessons in the book,
You'll see that most of them are true,
I found them out, and so will YOU!

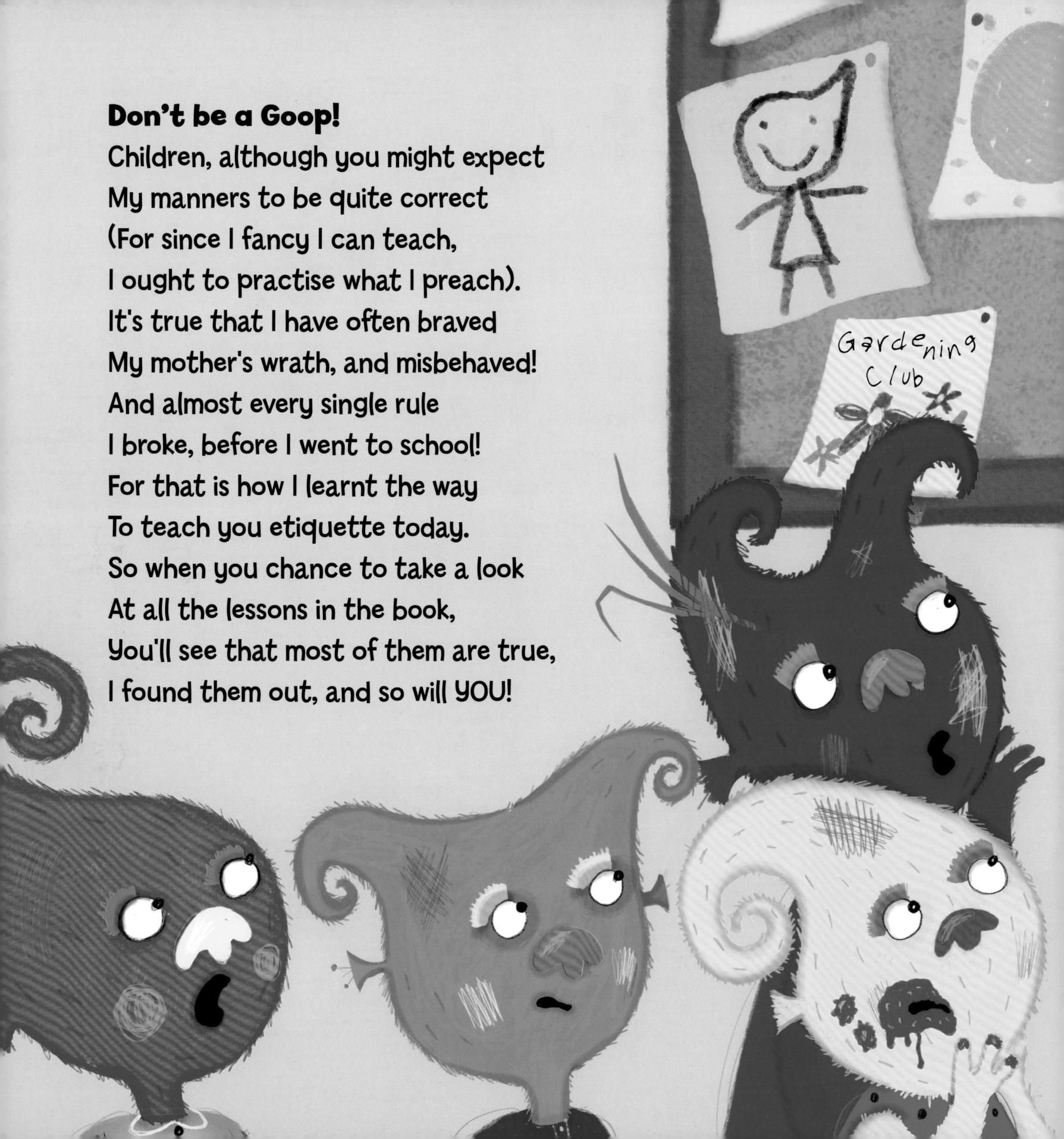

Gardening Club

Don't be a Goop!

Written by Frank Gelett Burgess
Illustrated by Maxine Lee

Licensed exclusively to Top That Publishing Ltd
Tide Mill Way, Woodbridge, Suffolk, IP12 1AP, UK
www.topthatpublishing.com
Copyright © 2014 Tide Mill Media
All rights reserved
0 2 4 6 8 9 7 5 3 1
Printed and bound in China

ISBN 978-1-78244-912-6

A catalogue record for this book is available from the British Library